Off in the country of the elephants
King Babar and Queen Celeste
are rejoicing :
they have signed a treaty of peace with the rhinoceros,
and their friend, the old lady,
has consented to remain with them.
She often tells the elephants children stories;
her little monkey, Zephir,
perched up in a tree,
also listens.

-3-

Leaving the old lady with Queen Celeste, Babar ha
with Cornelius, the oldest and wisest of
"This countryside is so beautiful that I woul
We must build
Our houses shall be on the shores of the
Zephir, who has followed them, would

one for a walk along the banks of the large lake
all the elephants, and he says to him,
ke to see it every day as I wake up.
ur city here.
ke, and shall be surrounded with flowers and birds."
ike to catch a butterfly he sees...

While chasing the butterfly,
Zephir meets his friend Arthur,
the young cousin of the King and Queen,
who was amusing himself hunting for snails.
All of a sudden, they see
one, two, three, four dromedaries
five, six, seven dromedaries
eight, nine, ten .....
There are more than they can count.
And the chief of the cavalcade calls to them:
"Can you please tell us where we can find King Babar?"

-6-

Escorted by Arthur and Zephir
The dromedaries have found Babar
They are bringing him all his heavy baggage
and all the things which he had bought
out in the big world,
during his honeymoon.
Babar thanks them:
"You must be tired, gentlemen.
Won't you rest under the shade of the palm trees?"
Then, turning to the old lady
and to Cornelius, he says:
"Now we will be able to build our city."

Having called an assembly of all the elephants,
Babar climbs up on a packing case, and,
in a loud voice proclaims the following words:
"My friends,
I have in these, trunks, these bales and these sacks,
gifts for each of you.
There are dresses, suits, hats and materials,
paint boxes, drums,
fishing tackle and rods, ostrich feathers,
tennis rackets and many other things.
I will divide all this among you
as soon as we have finished building our city.
This city – the city of the elephants –
I would like to suggest that we name Celesteville,
in honor of your Queen."
All the elephants raised their trunks and cried:
"What a good idea!
What an excellent idea!"

The elephants set to work quickly.
Arthur and Zephir hand out the tools.
Babar tells each one what he should do.
He marks with sign-boards
where the streets and houses should go.
He orders some to cut down trees,
some to move stones;
others saw wood or dig holes.
With what joy they all strive to do their best!
The Old Lady is playing the phonograph for them
and from time to time Babar plays on his trumpet;
He is fond of music.
All the elephants
are as happy as he is.
They drive nails, draw logs,
pull and push,
dig, fetch and carry,
opening their big ears wide as they work.

Over in the big lake
the fish are complaining among themselves:
"We can't even sleep peacefully any longer,"
they say.
"These elephants make the most dreadful noise!
What are they building?
When we jump out of the water
we really haven't time to see clearly.
We'll have to ask the frogs
what it is all about."

The birds also
gathered together
to discuss what the elephants were up to.
The pelicans and the flamingos,
the ducks and the ibis
and even the smaller birds
all twittered, chirrupped and quacked.
and the parrots enthusiastically kept repeating:
"Come and see Celesteville, the most beautiful of all citees!
Come and see Celesteville, the most beautiful of all cities!"

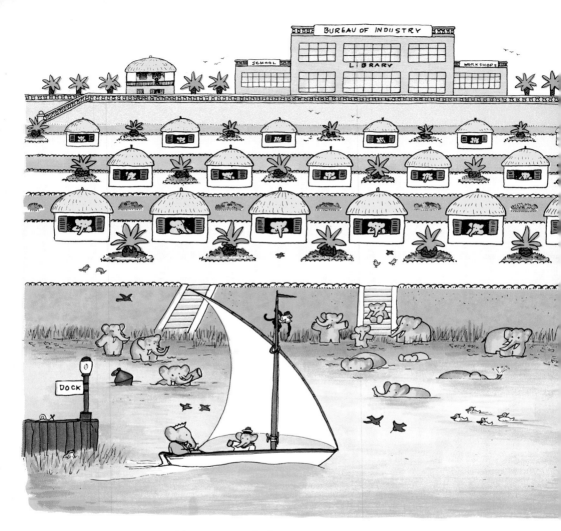

Here is Celesteville! The elephants have just
Babar goes for a sail with Arthur and Zephir.
                                    Each elephant
The Old Lady's is at the upper left, the one for
                                    The big lake is visible
The Bureau of Industry is next door to the Amuse

finished building it and are resting or bathing.
 He is well satisfied, and admires his new capital.
 has his own house.
the King and Queen is at the upper right.
 from all their windows.
ment Hall which will be very practical and convenient.

Today

Babar keeps his promise.
He gives a gift to each elephant
and also serviceable clothes suitable for work-days
and beautiful rich clothes for holidays.
After thanking their king most heartily,
the elephants all go home dancing with glee.

Babar has decided that next Sunday
all the elephants will dress up in their best clothes
and assemble in the gardens of the Amusement Park.
The gardeners have much to do.
They rake the paths,
water the flower beds
and set out the last flower pots.

The elephant children are planning a surprise
for Babar and Celeste.
They have asked Cornelius
to teach them
the song of the elephants.
Arthur had the idea.
They are very attentive,
keep time, and will know it perfectly by Sunday.

SONG OF THE ELEPHANTS

MELODY

Pa-ta- li di - ra-pa-ta crom-da crom-da ri-pa-lo

REFRAIN:

Pa-ta Ba-ta Ko Ko Ko - - - - - - - - - -

WORDS

1ST VERSE

PATALI DIRAPATA
CROMDA CROMDA RIPALO
PATA PATA
KO KO KO

2ND VERSE

BOKORO DIPOULITO
RONDI RONDI PEPINO
PATA PATA
KO KO KO

3RD VERSE

ÉMANA KARASSOLI
LOUCRA LOUCRA PONPONTO
PATA PATA
KO KO KO

NOTE: This song is the old chant of the Mammoths, Cornelius himself doesn't know what the words mean —

The cooks are hurriedly preparing
cakes and dainties of all kinds.,
Queen Celeste comes to help them.
Zephir comes too, with Arthur.
He tastes the vanilla cream
to see if it is just right;
first he puts in his finger, then his hand, and then his arm.
Arthur is dying of envy and would like to stick his trunk in it.

In order to have one last taste
Zephir bends his head, sticks out his tongue
and plouf — in he falls head first.
At this sound the chief cook looks around, and,
greatly annoyed, fishes him out by the tail.
The soup chef bursts out laughing. Arthur hides.
Poor little Zephir is a sight, all yellow and sticky.
Celeste scolds him and goes off to clean him up.

Sunday comes at last. In th
the elephants saunter about dressed magnificently. The childre
The cakes were delicious! What a wonderful day!
The Old Lady is already organizin

ardens of the Amusement Park
ave sung their song, Babar has kissed each one.
Unfortunately, it is over all too soon.
he last round of hide-and-seek.

The next day
after their morning dip in the lake,
the children go to school.
And they are glad to find their dear teacher, the Old Lady,
waiting for them.
Lessons are never tiresome
when she teaches.

After having settled the little ones at their tasks,
She turns her attention to the older ones, and asks them:
"Two times two?"_ "Three," answers Arthur.
"No, no, four," said his neighbor Ottilie.
"For, that's what we study for," sang Zephir.
"Four", repeated Arthur,
"I'll not forget that again, teacher."

All the elephants
who are too old to attend classes,
have chosen a trade.
For example:
Tapitor is a cobbler, Pilophage an officer,
Capoulosse is a doctor, Barbacol a tailor,
Podular a sculptor
and Hatchibombotar is a street-cleaner.
Doulamor is a musician, Olur is a mechanic,
Poutifour a farmer, Fandago is a learned man.
Justinien is a painter and Coco a clown.—
If Capoulosse has holes in his shoes,
he brings them to Tapitor, and,
if Tapitor is sick, Capoulosse takes care of him.
If Barbacol wants a statue for his mantle piece,
he asks Podular to carve one for him,
and when Podular's coat is worn out
Barbacol makes a new one to order for him.
Justinien paints a portrait of Pilophage
who will protect him against his enemies.
Hatchibombotar cleans the streets, Olur repairs the automobiles,
and, when they are all tired,
Doulamor plays his cello to entertain them.
After having settled grave problems,
Fandago relaxes and eats some of Poutifour's fruits.
As for Coco,
he keeps them all laughing
and gay.

TAPITOR

CAPOULOSSE   FANDAGO

BARBACOL

PODULAR

PILOPHAGE   JUSTINIEN

DOULAMOR

POUTIFOUR

HATCHIBOMBOTAR   OLUR

COCO

At Celesteville,
all the elephants work in the morning,
and in the afternoon they can do as they please.
They play, go for walks, read and dream...
Babar and Celeste
like to play tennis
with Mr. and Mrs. Pilophage.

Cornelius, Fandago, Podular and Capoulosse
prefer to play bowls.
The children play with
Coco, the clown.
Arthur and Zephir have put on masks,
There is also a shallow pool in which to sail their boats
and many other games besides.

But what the elephants like best of al

is the theatre in the Amusement Hall.

Every day, early in the morning,
Hatchibombotar sprinkles the streets
with his motor sprin`kler.
When Arthur and Zephir meet him,
they quickly take off their shoes,
and run after the car, barefoot.
"Oh what a fine shower!"
they say laughingly.
Unfortunately, Babar caught them at it one day.
"No dessert
for either of you, you rascals!"
he cried.

Arthur and Zephir are mischievous,
as are all little boys,
but they are not lazy.
Babar and Celeste visit the Old Lady,
and are amazed to hear them
play the violin and cello.
"It is wonderful!" said Celeste,
and Babar adds:
"My dear children, I am indeed pleased with you.
Go to the pastry shop
and select whatever cakes you like."

Arthur and Zephir are very happy
to have had all the cakes they wanted,
but they are even more delighted when
at the distribution of prizes,
they hear Cornelius read out:
"First prize for music:
a tie between Arthur and Zephir."
Very proudly, with wreaths on their heads,
they went back to their seats.
After having rewarded the good scholars,
Cornelius made a noble speech.

"... And now I wish you all a pleasant holiday!"
he ended up.
Everyone clapped hard and applauded loudly.
Then, quite weary, he sat down,
but alas and alack,
his fine hat was on the chair
and he crushed it completely.
"A regular pancake!" said Zephir.
Cornelius was aghast,
and sadly looked at what was left of his hat.
What would he wear on the next formal occasion?

The Old Lady promises Cornelius
to sew some plumes on his old derby,
and in order to console him further, she invites him
to go for a ride on the new merry-go-round
which Babar has just had built.

Podular has carved the animals,
  Justinien has painted them,
and the motor was installed by Olur.
  All three of them are very skillful.

  They have also made
the King's mechanical horse.
  Olur has just oiled it
  and Babar is winding it up.
He wants to give it a final trial
  before the big celebration
on the anniversary of the founding
  of Celesteville.

The weather was perfect, the day of the celebration. Arthur
Cornelius follows, his hat completely transformed.
All those who are not marching, are

marches at the head of the parade with Zephir and the band
Then come the soldiers and the trades companies.
watching this unforgetable spectacle.

1

Zephir
on his way home
from the celebration
notices a curious stick.

2

He goes to pick it up.
Horrors!
It is a snake
which rears its head and hisses,

3

and cruelly bites
the Old Lady
who tries to hide Zephir
in her arms.

4

Arthur furiously smashes
his bugle
on the snake's back
and kills him.

The Old Lady's arm
swells rapidly,
and she hastens
to the hospital.

Dr. Capoulosse
takes care of her,
and gives her
a hypodermic of serum.

Zephir
sadly remains
near his mistress.
She is very ill.

"I can't tell you
until tomorrow,
whether she will get well."
Capoulosse says to Babar.

As Babar leaves the hospital,
he hears cries of "Fire! Fire!"
Cornelius' house is on fire.
The stairway is already full of smoke;
the firemen succeed
in rescuing Cornelius,
but he is half suffocated
and a burning beam has injured him.
Capoulosse, summoned in great haste,
gives him first aid
before having him moved to the hospital.
A match
which Cornelius thought he had thrown into the ash-tray
but which had actually fallen,
still lighted in the trash-basket,
had been enough to start
this terrible fire.

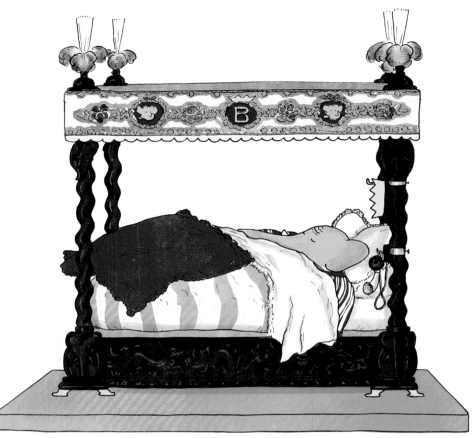

That night
when Babar goes to bed,
he shuts his eyes but cannot sleep.
"What a dreadful day!" he thinks.
"It began so well,
why did it have to end so badly?
Before these two accidents
we were all so happy and peaceful
at Celesteville!

We had forgotten that misfortune existed !
Oh my dear old Cornelius,
and you, dear Old Lady,
I would give my crown
to see you cured.
Capoulosse was to telephone me any news.
Oh ! How long this night seems,
and how worried I am ! "

. . . .

Babar finally drops off to sleep,
his sleep is restless and soon he dreams :
He hears a knocking on his door,
Tap ! Tap ! Tap !
then a voice says to him :
" It is I, Misfortune,
with some of my companions,
come to pay you a visit."
Babar looks out of the window,
and sees a frightful old woman
surrounded by flabby ugly beasts.
He opens his mouth to shout :
" Ugh ! Faugh ! Go away quickly ! "
But he stops to listen
to a very faint noise :
Frr ! Frr ! Frr !
as of birds
flying in a flock,
and he sees coming toward him . . . . .

.... graceful winged elephants
who chase Misfortune
away from Celesteville
and bring back
Happiness. —
At this point he awakes,
and feels ever so much better.

GOODNESS

FEAR

DESPAIR

INDOLENCE

MISFORTUNE

SICKNESS

ANGER

STUPIDITY

DISCOURAGEMENT

Babar dresses and runs to the hospital.
Oh joy! What does he see?
His two patients
walking in the garden
He can scarcely believe his eyes.
"We are all well again,"
says Cornelius,
"but all this excitement
has made me as hungry as a wolf.
Let's get some breakfast,
and then later we'll rebuild
my house."

- 46 -

A week later,
in Babar's drawing room,
The Old Lady says
to her two friends:
"Do you see how in this life
one must never be discouraged?
The vicious snake didn't kill me,
and Cornelius is completely recovered.
Let's work hard and cheerfully
and we'll continue
to be happy."

And since that day,
over in the elephants' country,
everyone has been happy
and contented. —